Laura leaned forward, a pleased look
"I heard that Mr. Bell asked Katie Shannon's mother
to help run the turnoff. Just because *she* doesn't like
to watch television, she doesn't want anyone else to
either."

Katie's face turned bright red. Jumping out of the
booth, she stomped over to Laura and stood in front
of her with her fists on her hips and her feet planted
wide.

*"Laura McCall! You don't know what you're talking
about!* That's not at all why my mother is organizing
the TV turnoff."

"Oh?" said Laura, looking like a cat that had just
swallowed a mouse. "She's probably not telling Mr.
Bell how to run the turnoff, either?"

"He asked for her help," snapped Katie, "and
she's helping. That's all! And not only that, I'm
helping, too!"

Katie couldn't believe what she had just said. She
had actually committed herself to working for the
turnoff when it was the last thing in the world she
wanted to do. Still, she thought desperately, what
else can I do?

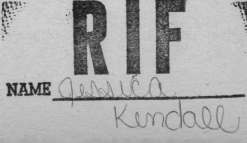

THE FABULOUS FIVE

The Great TV Turnoff

BETSY HAYNES

A BANTAM SKYLARK BOOK®
NEW YORK · TORONTO · LONDON · SYDNEY · AUCKLAND

RL 5, 009–012

THE GREAT TV TURNOFF
A Bantam Skylark Book / April 1991

ISBN 0-553-15861-9

Published simultaneously in the United States and Canada

PRINTED IN THE UNITED STATES OF AMERICA

CWO   0 9 8 7 6 5 4 3 ? 1

For Susan Johnasen Smith

CHAPTER

1

"Tony, did you hear that Derek Travelstead asked Tammy Lucero to go out for pizza last night?" Katie Shannon asked Tony Calcaterra. The two of them were sitting on the sofa in Tony's family room, along with some of Tony's other friends. A baseball game was on the television.

"Um hm," Tony mumbled, his eyes glued to the TV screen.

Katie frowned. He had barely heard her question. "I really can't see those two together," she continued. "Can you?"

"Right," Tony said absently.

1

Katie was getting more annoyed by the second. He was obviously more interested in a dumb baseball game than he was in her.

Narrowing her eyes, she asked, "What do you think about the situation on Mars? Do you think the *Grysnoks* or *Platybabies* will win the *Diddly Plop* tournament?"

Tony flashed her a quick smile. "Yeah, sure. *Hey, all right!*" he cried suddenly. "Did you guys see that?" He leapt off the sofa. "Did you see that play Canseco made? Man, he's out of sight."

Randy Kirwan pounded his fists on the floor, where he was stretched out on his stomach in front of the television. "He's the greatest. I bet he's the best player of all time."

"Naw," disagreed Keith Masterson, whose legs were dangling over the arm of an easy chair as he munched on a handful of potato chips. "Rickey Henderson is the greatest. He can even steal bases. Canseco can't keep up with him."

Katie rolled her eyes in frustration. Last Saturday night Tony had been so involved in a baseball game that was on TV that he had been late picking her up for their date. He'd been so late, in fact, that they had totally missed the movie. Because it was a thriller, the theater wouldn't admit anyone after it started. Katie had been terribly disappointed. She had really wanted to see the movie. Tony had apologized. He had promised her that in the future he wouldn't get so carried away with ball games on TV that he would forget about her, but it was happening again. She could hardly believe it!

Other than passing him a few times in the halls of Wakeman Junior High, she hadn't seen Tony all week. She had come to his house this Saturday afternoon hoping to spend some time alone with him. Instead she was sitting in a room full of boys watching a dumb baseball game on TV. Worse yet, he hadn't even heard her gibberish question.

"Tony!" she said, raising her voice.

"Yeah? Hey, look at that, Katie. Canseco's getting a standing ovation from the crowd. I love it! I *love* it!"

Katie got up and stomped out of the room. She pulled open the front door, then hesitated, hoping Tony would come after her.

Instead he just called, "You leaving, Katie? See you later."

She opened her mouth to reply just as a cheer went up in the family room. "Forget it," she muttered, then slammed the door behind her.

As she strode down the walk, she thought back angrily over the past week. In spite of his promise, it had been one baseball game after another. He hadn't come over to see her once, and now all he said when he saw her leaving was, "See you later." Well, she would show him. If he called her later to apologize, she wouldn't be home. Melanie Edwards's house wasn't far, and she jumped on her bike and headed there.

Mrs. Edwards greeted Katie at the door. "Hi, Katie. Melanie's in the living room watching TV."

"Hi, Mrs. Edwards. Thanks."

Melanie had been one of Katie's best friends ever since the two of them, along with Jana Morgan, Christie Winchell, and Beth Barry had formed The Fabulous Five when they were in fifth grade. Right now Katie needed to talk to someone about Tony, and there was no one who knew more about boys than Melanie.

Katie found her planted in a recliner.

"Hey, Katie. Come on in," Melanie called, looking up. "You've gotta watch this *Star Trek* rerun. The crew from the starship *Enterprise* finds some kids on this planet. Something has happened to the adults, and the kids live in these old buildings all by themselves. They can hardly remember grown-ups—they call them *grups*. I've seen it at least a dozen times, but I still love it. Can you imagine living in a world without grown-ups?"

"Sounds great," said Katie, settling into a chair. She

watched the show for a few minutes before bringing up Tony.

"Melanie, I've got a prob—" she began.

"Just a minute," Melanie interrupted. "This is a funny part. Watch what they do next."

Katie looked back at the screen, where the kids were running around like monkeys. It didn't seem that funny to her.

She tried again. "Melanie."

"Let's not talk until this is over, okay?" said Melanie, her eyes glued to the TV.

Katie sank back in her chair and stared at the screen. What in the world was so special about this program that two friends couldn't even talk? It looked like just another dumb TV show to her. Katie knew that Melanie was hooked on soap operas, but she hadn't realized she was hooked on *Star Trek* reruns, too.

"I've gotta go," said Katie. "I'll see you later."

"See you," responded Melanie, waving good-bye without taking her eyes off the television.

"I'm home!" called Katie as she walked in the front door.

"Hi, sweetheart," returned her mother from her office.

Katie was tempted to go talk to her mom, but she knew if Willie was in her office, that meant she was busy working on a free-lance writing assignment and didn't want to be disturbed. Katie's dad had died when she was little, and her mother worked hard to support both of them.

Katie threw her jacket on a chair and headed upstairs. She flopped backward on her bed and took a deep breath, wishing she had someone to talk to.

Christie! she thought. I'll call Christie. Why didn't I think of her sooner?

Christie's mother answered the phone.

"This is Katie, Mrs. Winchell. Is Christie there?"

"Yes she is, but she's watching a National Geographic special on television for a school science project and can't come to the phone right now. Do you want me to have her call you?"

"Oh . . . yes. When she gets time, please." Katie hung up the phone dejectedly.

She felt like one of the kids on the show Melanie had been watching, but instead of the *grups* disappearing, all her friends had disappeared, mostly to TV land.

The urge to talk to someone grew stronger, and

Katie wandered into the little spare bedroom that served as her mother's office.

"Hi, honey," Willie said as she made a note on a yellow pad of paper next to her computer before turning to Katie. "Hey, why the long face?"

Katie shrugged.

"Come on now, sweetheart. This is your mom. If anyone can tell when something's bothering you, it's me." Her mother listened closely as Katie told her about her day.

"Sometimes I think television should be banned," said Katie.

Willie nodded sympathetically. "You mentioned a unit on television and the family in your Family Living class. Has the teacher discussed any of the harmful effects of watching too much TV?"

Katie shook her head. "Nope. We've mostly talked about good and bad programs. My teacher, Mrs. Clark, talks about violence on TV, what's good for children to watch, stuff like that."

"Is that all?" asked Willie, looking concerned. "Doesn't she ever talk about TV's becoming a substitute for human interaction? Or how it can affect basic family relationships?"

Katie glanced at her mother in surprise and said, "No."

Mom has that fiery look in her eyes again, she thought. The one that usually triggers a protest of some sort, or a newspaper article.

"Well, that's ridiculous!" her mother cried. "The teachers ought to be showing you kids that *not* watching television is far better than trying to decide which programs are okay to watch and which aren't. I'm surprised there isn't a TV turnoff project in your Family Living class."

"A TV turnoff?" echoed Katie. "What's that?"

"It's when all the kids in a class and their families turn off their television sets for a week or more," Willie explained. "In fact, sometimes entire schools do a TV turnoff."

"They do?" Katie asked incredulously. "They don't watch any television *at all*?"

"None," her mother replied emphatically. "In fact," she added, waving her pencil at Katie, "the junior high school in Branford had a TV turnoff just last month. It was a great success. Did you hear about it?"

Katie shook her head. Branford was a small nearby town, and Branford Junior High was one of Wakeman's biggest rivals in sports. Still, Katie hadn't heard anything about a TV turnoff.

Willie looked as if she were miles away. "I ought to drive up to Branford and interview the people involved," she said slowly, as if the idea were still forming in her mind. "Then I could write an article about their project for our local paper and suggest that Wakeman Junior High students do a TV turnoff of their own."

A little tingle of fear ran up Katie's spine. She hadn't really meant it when she'd said TV should be banned. She was just angry at Tony and Melanie. But now Willie was talking about having a huge TV turnoff at Wakeman Junior High. If the kids at Wacko couldn't watch TV for a whole week or more, they'd be furious. Even worse, Katie thought miserably, they'd be furious at me!

"Mo-om," Katie pleaded softly. But as she glanced at her mother, who was busily making notes on a legal pad, she had a feeling of impending doom.

CHAPTER

2

*K*atie forgot all about her mother's new project until she picked up the newspaper the next Saturday afternoon. Willie's article took up the entire lower half of the front page.

The headline blared: BRANFORD TELEVISION TURNOFF A HUGE SUCCESS. Underneath that, in smaller letters, was: Similar Turnoff Suggested for Wakeman Junior High. Even worse, her mother's byline was on the story, for all the world to see.

Katie groaned as she skimmed the article. Willie called television one of the greatest menaces in society today, and she quoted people who said that watching too much TV was ruining the lives of children. Then she went on to report that several people in Branford who had taken part in the turnoff said that it was the best thing that had happened to them in a long time. The article ended with a plea to Mr. Bell and the teachers at Wakeman to conduct their own turnoff.

Katie let the paper drop into her lap. Oh, please, not Wakeman Junior High, she prayed fervently. The kids at Wacko will blame *me*. They'll burn me at the stake like Joan of Arc. They'll push me off a bridge—if they can find one high enough. Tony won't like me much, either, if he can't watch his precious baseball games.

"Oh, brother," Katie muttered. "This is all I need. I just hope that nobody—I mean, *nobody*—reads it."

"I saw your mom's article in the paper today," said Jana that evening as The Fabulous Five stood in front of the ticket booth at the movie theater in the mall.

"So did I," said Christie.

"I'd hate to be in your shoes if Mr. Bell decides Wacko ought to follow her suggestion and do a TV turnoff," Beth chimed in, giving Katie a sympathetic look. "On the other hand," she added quickly, "I'd hate to be in my shoes, too, now that I'm in the Media Club and we have our own weekly TV program. A turnoff would mean that nobody in Wakeman could watch our show. Your mom wouldn't do a thing like that, would she?"

Katie shrugged. "I'm really worried. You know my mom when she gets on a campaign, and she's all fired up over this TV issue. She thinks everyone would benefit from a TV turnoff."

"How could I possibly benefit?" Beth demanded. "I'm learning all about television production, as well as how to become a performer. My whole future is at stake."

Katie was beginning to feel trapped. "Hey, it's only for a week," she argued.

Melanie's expression was one of horror. "I can't miss my soaps for a week. How would I know what's happening to the people on *Interns and Lovers*? I'd die. Especially now that I have an autographed poster of Jason Rider, the star. I mean, I'd feel *disloyal*."

"Oh, Melanie, don't be silly," said Christie. "You could just tape the show every day, the way you do anyway. Then you could pig out on a whole week of *Interns and Lovers* one day when the turnoff's over. Just think, five straight hours of *Interns and Lovers*. You'd love that."

"I don't want to watch five straight hours of *Interns*

and Lovers," complained Melanie. "I want to watch what's going on while it's really happening."

Christie rolled her eyes in disbelief. "What's going on in the lives of the people on *Interns and Lovers* isn't real, Mel. They're just characters someone dreamed up."

"To me they're real," said Melanie, sticking out her lower lip. "The characters seem like friends." She turned to Katie. "Why does your mother want to get involved, anyway?"

"Right," said Beth. "Why does she care if kids watch a lot of TV?"

"She says television is an addiction that keeps people from living in the real world," Katie replied.

"See, Melanie." Jana laughed. "You're an addict."

Melanie stuck her tongue out at Jana. "I am not an addict. Watching television is a great American pastime. Besides, I'm not the only one who watches TV. You guys all do, too."

"I don't watch that much television," declared Jana proudly.

"Me, either," said Christie. "And I think your mother's right. People do watch too much TV."

"When I called your house last weekend you were watching television, too," said Katie.

"That was different," protested Christie. "I needed

to watch it for a school project. Does your mother disapprove of that, too?"

Katie didn't know what to say. She was starting to get tired of defending her mother. Just then she noticed Laura McCall and her three best friends, Melissa McConnell, Tammy Lucero, and Funny Hawthorne, standing nearby. Laura called her clique The Fantastic Foursome, and they had been The Fabulous Five's biggest rivals since the beginning of the school year.

"Who cares if more homes in America have TV sets than have toilets?" Laura was saying. She was pretending to talk to her friends, but she was speaking so loudly that Katie knew she was supposed to hear. The statement about TV sets and toilets was from Katie's mother's article.

Katie moved in closer to Jana and tried to ignore Laura.

"Personally I'm glad that I'll get to watch three hundred and fifty thousand commercials by the time I finish high school." Melissa's voice was sarcastic and just as loud as Laura's. "I just *love* commercials!"

The four girls laughed as if Melissa had cracked a hilarious joke. Katie bristled.

"Some people's *mothers* should mind their own business," said Tammy Lucero.

Katie whirled around and started toward The Fantastic Foursome, but Jana reached out and grabbed her arm. "Cool it, Katie," she whispered. "You know they're just trying to get to you. If you go over there, you'll be playing right into their hands."

"I don't care," Katie mumbled. "Tammy was talking about my mother." She pulled against Jana's hand.

"Look, Katie. There's Tony," said Melanie.

Katie looked around eagerly. Tony was standing near the first-floor escalator with Shane Arrington and Bill Soliday. Since the center of the mall served as the lobby of the theater, it was impossible to tell if the boys were planning to attend the movie or not.

Just then Tony saw her and waved. Katie immediately waved back.

"He's probably planning to sit with you," Melanie said.

Katie glanced through the crowd again, but Tony was talking to Shane and Bill now. She had first met him when she was selected to be a judge on Wakeman's Teen Court. He had had to appear before the court because of the earring he wore to school. At first she had thought he was totally macho and a troublemaker, but she had gradually come to see he wasn't that way at all.

Looking back at Melanie, she smiled and said, "I hope so."

As the crowd near the ticket booth grew, Katie lost sight of Tony.

"We'd better go in if we're going to get popcorn before the movie starts," said Beth, looking at her watch.

"Good idea," Katie agreed. "Tony can find me inside if he wants to."

Once The Fabulous Five were in their seats, Katie kept her eyes on the entrance, watching for Tony and his friends. That way, she reasoned, she could make sure he found her. Lots of Wacko kids came in. Some of them noticed her and waved. But when the lights dimmed, Tony and his friends still hadn't come into the theater. Where could they be? she wondered.

As the movie started, Katie sat on her legs to make herself taller as she scanned the faces in the darkened theater.

"Katie! Sit down," Taffy Sinclair whispered angrily. She was sitting in the row behind The Fabulous Five with Cory Dillon.

"Yes, *please*," said Shawnie Pendergast, who was seated next to them with her new boyfriend, Craig Meachem. "We can't see."

Katie slouched down in her seat. Next she tried peeking between people's heads, but every time she turned around, Taffy and Shawnie frowned at her.

Maybe the boys came in late, she thought, and they

sat in the back because they didn't want to trample on people's feet. Probably he'll be waiting for me in the mall when the movie's over, she decided. The idea made her feel better, and she settled back to watch the movie.

Katie looked around the lobby expectantly as the movie let out. She couldn't help feeling depressed as she scanned the crowded mall. Tony was nowhere to be seen.

"Come on, guys," said Jana. "Let's go to Taco Plenty for a soda."

As they followed the crowd through the mall toward the fast-food restaurant, the girls passed an electronic appliance store. Katie glanced in and stopped in her tracks. There, sitting on the floor in the middle of a semicircle of television sets all showing the same baseball game, sat Tony, Shane, and Bill.

CHAPTER

3

Katie raced down to the kitchen the next morning to talk to her mother. She had tossed and turned all night, thinking about the possibility of a turnoff and the consequences it would bring to her life. There was no question that she wanted to get Tony away from his TV for a while, but she was convinced that this wasn't the way to do it.

"Mom, I know you really believe in this whole business of television being bad for kids," she began, "but think about what it will do to me. I won't just be the most unpopular girl in Wakeman. I'll be the most *hated* girl in Wakeman."

Willie smiled and stirred her coffee. "I'm sure some kids will be upset for a couple of days, but it won't be as bad as you think. Besides, you always have your friends in The Fabulous Five to stick by you until the worst blows over."

"Humpft," snorted Katie. "Beth's mad because no one will get to see the Media Club's big cable TV production on Saturday morning. She says her entire future is at stake. And Melanie is hooked on a soap opera, and she says she'll die if she has to miss five episodes."

Willie chuckled. "Nobody's going to die without TV, believe me. Besides, Mr. Bell may not even be interested in my idea."

"I should be so lucky," Katie mumbled. There was no use talking to her mother about it anymore.

Katie thought over that conversation with her mother as she headed to school Monday morning. There was a possibility that Mr. Bell wouldn't be interested in a TV turnoff, of course, but she couldn't count on it. She also couldn't count on the total support of The Fabulous Five. Beth and Melanie were definitely against it, and Jana and Christie hadn't actually said they were for it. She might have to face the anger of the entire school all alone.

She ducked onto the school ground and headed for The Fabulous Five's meeting place by the fence. She kept her eyes down, hoping no one would notice her and get on her case about the article.

Christie and Melanie were waiting at the fence.

"Wow, has your mother really started something," said Melanie the moment Katie reached them. "The TV turnoff is all everybody's talking about."

Katie let out a sigh of exasperation. "It was just one measly article," she argued. "Probably nothing will come of it."

"I hope you're right," said Melanie, shaking her head doubtfully.

"I agree with you, Katie," said Christie. "I mean, it isn't as if she went to the school board and demanded a turnoff, or anything. Maybe Mr. Bell didn't even read her article."

Just then Beth came rushing up with Dekeisha Adams.

"Hey, you guys," called Dekeisha. "Big trouble."

Beth was nodding. "We don't know what's going on, but we just walked by the media center, and Mr. Bell and all the teachers are having some kind of meeting in there."

"The teachers never meet in the morning before school unless it's some kind of emergency," said Dekeisha. "I'll bet it's about that article your mother wrote, Katie. I'll bet they're talking about a television turnoff for Wakeman Junior High. All I have to say is, I hope it doesn't happen."

Katie wished the ground would open up and swallow her. Everyone was looking at her. Even her best friends.

"Maybe the meeting's about something else," she offered weakly. "I mean, just because my mom wrote an article . . ."

Fortunately the first bell rang before Katie had to say anymore. She headed for her locker, wishing she could climb into it and hide there for the rest of the day. Dekeisha was probably right, she thought. Why else would the teachers be having a special meeting this morning? They must be talking about a TV turnoff. And I'm going to get all the blame!

Katie held her breath when Miss Simone, the school secretary, made the morning announcements over the loudspeaker during home room. There were the usual things mentioned, such as after-school activities and the lunch menu, but there was nothing about a turnoff.

She breathed a sigh of relief. Maybe she had been worrying for nothing.

Still she couldn't relax. All morning long she felt as if every kid in school were looking at her. When the lunch bell finally rang, she hurried to the cafeteria to meet her friends.

"Anyone hear anything about the teachers' meeting?" she asked as she sat down with her tray.

"Not yet," said Beth. She lowered her voice and frowned. "But everybody's betting it's about the *you-know-what*."

Suddenly Beth's expression changed to surprise, and she cleared her throat loudly. Without moving her lips she said, "Katie, don't look now, but I think Tony's heading this way."

Katie inhaled sharply and sat up straight. "Oh, my gosh," she whispered.

"Yo there, Your Honor," came a familiar voice from behind her. "Got a minute?"

Katie composed herself the best she could and turned around. "Sure," she mumbled.

Tony gestured toward an empty table. "We can talk over there. So what's been happening?" he asked as soon as she sat down beside him. "I haven't seen much of you lately."

Katie blinked in surprise. What's been happening?

Was that all he had to say? What's been happening, she wanted to scream, is that you've been acting like a total jerk!

He didn't wait for her reply. "Say, Katie," he continued. "Is it okay if I come over tonight?"

"Tonight?" she asked, her spirits soaring. Maybe she had been wrong about him.

"Yeah. The White Sox are playing the Yankees. Our TV set's broken, and I thought you and I could watch on yours. Now I know you get mad when I spend too much time watching baseball, but it ought to be a super game. Even you'd enjoy watching it."

"You've got to be kidding!" Katie exploded. "If there's one thing I do *not* want to do, it's watch another stupid ball game on TV."

Tony looked flabbergasted. He opened his mouth to respond, but Katie wasn't finished yet.

"Not only that, I'm glad your set is broken. That's all you seem to care about anymore. Television, *television*, *TELEVISION*. You've forgotten I'm even alive. And that's not all, you're turning into a television addict!"

Katie stood up and whirled around, marching back to the table where her friends sat staring at her. Katie winced. She hadn't meant to shout. Probably everyone had heard her blow up at Tony.

"Wow, Katie," said Jana. "I think he knows you're mad at him now."

"So does the whole cafeteria," said Christie.

"What is he doing?" asked Katie, suddenly worried that she had gone too far.

"He's outta here," said Beth. "Gone like a flash. Uh-oh," she added. "Here come Laura and her troops. I have to hand it to you, Katie. When you blow it, you do it right."

Katie stiffened as Laura McCall and her friends stopped beside the table.

Laura looked at Katie through narrowed eyes. "And here I thought everything was your mother's fault."

"What are you talking about?" demanded Katie.

"You know what I'm talking about," said Laura. "Trying to tell the kids at Wakeman that they can't watch TV."

Katie stared right back at her. "My mother's not trying to tell anyone anything. She just had a good idea and wrote an article about it. That's all."

"It sounds like a dumb idea to me," said Laura. "And I don't think for a minute that anyone will go along with it. Why don't you tell your mother to stay out of Wakeman's business if she hasn't got any better ideas than that one?" She flipped the end of her long braid as she talked.

Katie fumed. "It is not a dumb idea," she fired back. "In fact, more and more I think it's a great idea."

"Are you sure you didn't think of it yourself?"

The question threw Katie for a moment.

Laura watched Katie hesitate, and the corners of her mouth curled in a little smile. "Of course it was your idea, Katie Shannon. And you proved it to everybody a few minutes ago. You're afraid you're losing Tony, aren't you? He's paying more attention to television than to you. You said so yourself. You can't kid us. You cooked up this whole idea to get your boyfriend back."

"Wha—I—," Katie sputtered.

Before she could get any words out, Laura turned to her friends and commanded, "Let's go."

Katie stared after Laura and her friends as they sailed out the cafeteria door.

CHAPTER

4

*K*atie was miserable all afternoon. In the halls other students glared at her, and she couldn't help thinking about all the rumors Laura and her friends were spreading. And then there was her problem with Tony. She didn't have the slightest idea what to do about him.

Finally, last period arrived. It was a relief to watch Mr. Naset write historical dates on the board and know that she could go home soon.

Katie's thoughts were interrupted by the public address speaker over Mr. Naset's desk as it crackled to life.

27

"Attention, students and teachers," said Miss Simone. "Mr. Bell has a special announcement."

Katie sank low in her seat as the kids in her class began shuffling and looking at each other. She had a feeling that she knew what was coming, and she wished she could become invisible.

"Students, faculty," Mr. Bell began. "I'm issuing a very exciting challenge to each and every one of you." There was a slight pause as he cleared his throat and went on. "As I'm sure some of you know, the junior high school in Branford has just completed a very successful television turnoff. The students, the faculty, and their families all agreed to give up watching TV for one week. We've been discussing the idea of a TV turnoff at Wakeman, and we think it has merit. Besides the fact that it would be a terrific challenge, it would give us all a chance to do things some of us haven't done for a while because we've been sitting in front of the boob tube."

Mr. Bell paused again, and this time angry grumbles sounded across the room. Katie looked around nervously. Three or four kids were giving her dirty looks.

"Now, I know you all are aware that Branford beat us once in football and *twice* in basketball this year," Mr. Bell continued, as several kids in Katie's class booed. "And I know none of you would like to see Branford Junior High get ahead of us."

There was a pause, and this time a few students actually nodded.

"Consequently, I was so sure of the support of my students and faculty that I called the principal of Branford myself and told him to step aside for Wakeman Junior High. In order to prove our superiority, I am challenging you to turn off your television sets for not one—but *two whole weeks*! The turnoff will begin on Friday. We'll call the newspapers and radio stations. And we'll prove to Branford that Wakeman Junior High can't be beaten! Are you with me?"

The room was so silent that Katie could hear her heart beating. Then the grumbling started up again.

"No TV?" Derek Travelstead asked incredulously. "Is he kidding or what?"

"No, Derek," Mr. Naset said sternly. "He is not kidding. He hopes that everyone will have enough school spirit to want to join the program."

"Come on, everybody!" shouted Richie Corrierro. "Let's show those sissies at Branford what Wacko kids are made of!"

"Yeah," called Tony Sanchez. "They did one lousy week. Big deal! We can do two with our eyes shut!"

"You don't have to shut your eyes," said Shawnie Pendergast. "Just turn off your television."

The whole class laughed.

"Who wants to turn off their TV?" protested Tammy Lucero, glaring at Katie. "Just because they were dumb enough to do it at Branford doesn't mean we have to."

"I like TV," said Geena McNatt. "I don't see why the school wants to mess with what we watch, anyway." A few kids mumbled their agreement.

"It wasn't the *school's* idea," Tammy assured her. This time at least half the class gave Katie dirty looks.

When the dismissal bell rang, Katie headed straight for home without even stopping at her locker. She had more important things on her mind than the books she needed for homework. Her worst nightmare had just come true. People just didn't want to go along with a TV turnoff. They hated the idea. More than anything else, she needed to talk to Willie.

Katie stopped in the doorway to her mother's office. Willie was concentrating on her computer screen and didn't notice her at first. Katie took a couple of deep breaths and reminded herself that she had to stay calm, no matter how upset she felt. Finally she stepped inside and stopped beside her mother's desk.

Willie looked up from her typing. "Hi, sweetheart."

"I need to talk to you," Katie said urgently. "Okay?"

"Ooh." Willie raised her eyebrows. "Sounds important."

"It is important. It's about the TV turnoff." Katie could hear her own voice rising in anger, but she couldn't stop. "You started it! Now you've got to do something to stop it!"

"Whoa!" said Willie, looking startled. "Will you please calm down and tell me what you're talking about?"

Katie took another deep breath. She usually got along pretty well with Willie. But then, Willie had never done anything quite like this before.

"Just before school was out this afternoon, Mr. Bell made an announcement over the loudspeaker that Wakeman is going to do a TV turnoff, and not for just one week. For two! No one wants to do it, and they're all mad at *me*."

Willie sighed deeply. "I'm sorry everyone's blaming you, sweetheart," she said. "I knew about the turnoff. Mr. Bell called a little while ago to say that he had talked to the PTA and to his staff, and that the PTA is behind the turnoff one hundred percent. Most of his staff is, too. He told the teachers that if any of them are planning to use a television program for a class assignment, they should put it off for a while. He also assigned Mrs. Karl to be the school coordinator, and she's very enthusiastic about it. She's planning to come up with some ideas to get the students excited about the project."

"Big deal," grumbled Katie. She gave her mother a skeptical look. "It will take more than ideas from Mrs. Karl to get kids at Wacko excited about a television turnoff."

"Katie, I know you're worried about the other kids, but the turnoff will only be for two weeks. Your classmates should be able to do without TV for that long. And it will do them good to find out they can live without it."

"But, Mom," Katie protested. "You don't understand. Laura McCall says *I* started it because Tony spends more time watching television than he does with me. She says I'm afraid I'm losing my boyfriend, and the turnoff is my way of trying to get him back."

Willie sat up straight. "Well, you just tell her that you had nothing to do with it," she said indignantly. "Tell her that it was *my* idea. You've stood up to Laura before, sweetheart."

"Actually she's saying that you and I are in it together and that you should stay out of other people's business. See, Mom?" Katie pleaded. "It's a total disaster."

Willie took both of Katie's hands in hers and looked her daughter straight in the eyes. "You know I didn't write that article to embarrass you, don't you?"

Katie nodded and tried to swallow the lump in her throat.

"And you know that I only get involved in things like this because I believe in them, don't you?"

Katie nodded again.

"Then try to believe me when I say that everything is going to work out okay."

Shrugging, Katie mumbled, "Sure, Mom," and left the room. She wanted to believe her mother, but how could she? This was going to be the most miserable two weeks of her life.

CHAPTER

5

*W*hen Katie heard the telephone ring later that evening, she looked up from her homework. Maybe it was Tony, calling to say he really wanted to come over, but *not* to watch a baseball game on TV.

"Katie, it's for you," her mother shouted from the bottom of the stairs.

Taking the steps two at a time, Katie hurried to the phone, rehearsing as she went how sweet and forgiving she would be when Tony admitted he had been wrong.

"Hi, Katie. It's me, Jana."

"Oh . . . hi," Katie said in a small voice.

Jana chuckled. "Sorry to disappoint you. Who were you expecting?"

"Tony," Katie said with a sigh. "I was hoping he'd had time to think about our argument in the cafeteria today and was calling to say he was sorry."

"Don't count on it. I hate to be the bearer of bad news, but he's really steamed at you. That's what I called to tell you."

Katie swallowed hard. "What do you mean?"

"Well," Jana began, "you didn't come to Bumpers after school, but Tony was there. He and Randy and Shane sat with The Fabulous Five. And get this, he thinks you started this whole turnoff thing just to get back at him for watching so many baseball games on TV."

"He what!" Katie cried.

"You heard me," said Jana. "He said that you're the most stubborn person he's ever met and that he wouldn't put it past you. Those were his exact words."

"You're kidding! Why, how could he?" Katie sputtered in exasperation. "Jana, I can't believe he said that."

"Believe it," Jana said softly. "Anyway, I thought you ought to know. What are you going to do? Call him?"

"No way," Katie huffed. "I wouldn't call him now if my life depended on it."

"Oh, come on, Katie," said Jana. "Don't be so stubborn. You two are never going to work this out if you don't talk about it."

"Now *you're* calling me stubborn. What is this, some kind of conspiracy?"

"Sorry, Katie," answered Jana. "I was just trying to be a friend and tell you what Tony was saying. I've got to go now. I'll see you in the morning."

Katie stared at the telephone after she hung up. What was wrong with everybody, anyway?

When Katie got to school the next morning, she was not surprised at the number of students who had something to say about the turnoff.

"I'll do it, but I'm not happy about it," Mandy McDermott said, as Katie stopped beside a group of girls at the drinking fountain. "I don't really watch that much television, but I hate being told what I can and can't do."

"I watch lots," admitted Lisa Snow. "But I think it will be fun in a way. There are tons of things I keep meaning to do, but most of the time I just cop out and turn on the TV instead."

"Right," Alexis Duvall added, nodding, "and my parents are always calling me a couch potato."

"What I'm worried about is homework," said Dekeisha. "I always do homework in front of the television. I don't know why exactly. Maybe I just like the background noise."

"Hey, Katie, how do you feel about giving up TV?" asked Mandy. "I mean, it's your mother who started all this."

Katie swallowed hard, wishing desperately that she didn't have to answer. How could she explain to her friends that the whole idea for the turnoff had actually started when she had gotten angry at Tony for watching too much TV and had complained to her mother? She couldn't, that was all there was to it. "I . . . I don't really watch a lot of TV, either," she fumbled.

Alexis frowned. "Then you probably think this is a great idea."

"Yeah," added Mandy. "It's nothing to you if everyone else is miserable without TV."

"That's not true," Katie began, and then stopped. The only way she could defend herself would be to put all the blame on her mother. That would be an invitation for the others to bad-mouth Willie, and no matter how she felt about the turnoff, she couldn't let that happen. Throwing up her hands in frustration, she stomped away.

*　*　*

When Katie and Melanie arrived at Bumpers, Jana and Christie were saving seats. The fast-food restaurant had gotten its name from the brightly colored carnival bumper cars that were placed around the room for kids to sit in. The place was crowded with boys and girls, and the old Wurlitzer jukebox was blaring away.

"Where's Beth?" asked Melanie.

"The Media Club's having a meeting after school," said Jana. "She said she'd be here later."

"Anyone want anything?" Melanie asked. "Shane's at the counter, so I'm going to get a soda."

"I'll take one, too," said Katie, digging in her purse for money.

Melanie came back shortly with Shane and Randy Kirwan. Katie looked around for Tony. He wasn't there. She had an empty feeling in the pit of her stomach that it was because he didn't want to see her.

"So, Shane," said Christie. "What's going on with Igor these days?" Igor was Shane's iguana.

"He was tired when I left for school today. *Night of the Iguana* was on the late movies last night, and he stayed up to watch it. There were popcorn kernels all over his cage this morning."

The Fabulous Five laughed.

"Hey, Katie, is it true that there's no more TV for Wacko kids for the rest of the year?" Randy asked.

Katie's backbone went rigid.

"Yeah, I heard that, too," said Shane. "If it happens, I'm going to have to have a long talk with Igor. He loves TV, especially *Late Night With David Letterman*. He'd hate giving it up. But that's okay. The light from his TV has been keeping me awake, anyway."

"Laura's spreading that rumor," said Katie. "She's even saying that it was my idea, but it wasn't."

"What about video games?" asked Shane, looking at Katie. "Does that count as watching television?"

Katie shrugged. She hadn't thought about video games. "I don't know."

Shane looked puzzled. "If we can't watch television and we can't play video games, what's left in life?"

Shane and Randy looked at each other. "School?" they asked in unison.

"Aagh!" cried Randy, acting as if he were hanging himself.

"As far as I'm concerned, until somebody tells me otherwise, video games aren't part of the turnoff," Shane declared emphatically. "Hey, look. Here come Jon and Scott." He nodded toward Jon Smith and Scott Daly, who had just walked in the door. "Let's see if they want to play video games Saturday."

"Boy, Laura's not wasting any time starting rumors," mumbled Melanie, after the boys had left.

"Well, if that's all she does, sooner or later everyone will know she wasn't telling the truth," said Jana. "Most kids probably don't believe her, anyway."

"Geena did," said Katie. "She heard Laura's rumor that no one can watch television for the rest of the school year, too, and she thought it was true until I straightened her out."

Katie glanced up just as Beth walked into Bumpers and headed straight for them.

"Hi, everybody." Beth plopped down in the seat next to Jana. "Boy, have I got something to tell you. Jack Albright, the star of that new hit TV series *Taking Chances* is coming to town, and the Media Club is going to have a chance to interview him for the local cable station. Mr. Levine wants *me* to be the one to interview him. Can you believe that?" Her eyes were dancing. "Connie Chung, eat your heart out!"

"Oh, wow!" exclaimed Melanie. "I'd die if I got to be in the same room with Jack Albright."

"Gee, that is great, Beth," said Christie. "When's the interview?"

"Next Wednesday. A week from tomorrow."

"You're not planning on a new outfit for the interview, right?" Jana asked, grinning. The last time Beth had been on television with the Media Club, she had borrowed Shawnie Pendergast's credit card to buy new clothes and spent a fortune. "No new wardrobe," said Beth sheepishly. "But I'm dying to meet Jack Albright. He's such a great actor." Then Beth's smile faded. "There's one problem, though. The interview will probably be shown on cable television during the turn-off. You might as well know right now that if that happens, I'm going to cheat and watch myself on TV."

Katie swallowed and looked at Beth, not knowing what to say. She could understand Beth's position, but The Fabulous Five always stuck together. How could her own mother have started something that was going to split them apart?

Katie suddenly became aware of a nearby conversation.

"Can you imagine such a dumb thing?" Laura Mc-Call was saying to Daphne Alexandrou, Shelly Bramlett, and Holly Davis, who were sitting in a yellow bumper car about ten feet away. "This used to be a free country, but now we're being *forced* to turn off our television sets and leave them off. And it's all one person's fault," Laura reminded them.

"It's going to be tough," said Daphne, "but it will be a challenge, too. And I'd love to beat Branford. They've really been rubbing it in about beating us so many times in sports this year."

Holly nodded. "I have a cousin in Branford. She

said that they don't care who else they beat as long as they beat Wakeman. It would serve them right."

"I already know what's going to happen at our house," said Shelly. "My brother will have more time to pick on me, and I'll fight back. My mom'll be out of her mind by the end of the two weeks."

Laura leaned forward, a pleased look on her face. "Plus I heard that Mr. Bell asked Katie Shannon's mother to help run the turnoff. Just because *she* doesn't like to watch television, she doesn't want anyone else to, either. I bet she has lots of other great ideas for us, too."

Katie's face turned bright red, and little explosions went off in her brain. Jumping out of the booth, she stomped over to Laura and stood in front of her with her fists on her hips and her feet planted wide.

"*Laura McCall! You don't know what you're talking about!* That's not at all why my mother is organizing the TV turnoff."

"Oh?" said Laura, looking like a cat that had just swallowed a mouse. "She's probably not telling Mr. Bell how to run the turnoff, either?"

"He asked for her help," snapped Katie, "and she's helping. That's all! And not only that, I'm helping, too!"

Katie couldn't believe what she had just said. She had

actually committed herself to working for the turnoff when it was the last thing in the world she wanted to do. Still, she thought desperately, what else could I do?

CHAPTER

6

"What's that?" asked Dekeisha Adams, as a crowd gathered around the bulletin board outside the school office the next morning. Katie had to bounce on the tips of her toes to see.

"It's a notice about a school assembly for the TV turnoff on Friday," Marcie Bee called from the front of the crowd.

Dekeisha's face lit up, and she nudged Katie, saying, "Hey, an assembly means we can get out of class for one whole period. Maybe this turnoff isn't such a bad idea after all."

Everyone laughed, and Marcie went on, "It says that

anyone who wants to perform a skit, read a poem, or do anything that has to do with turning off television can participate in the assembly."

"Does that include people who are against the turn-off?" asked Taffy Sinclair. "If it does, maybe I'll do something."

Katie looked at Taffy in surprise. She had been a real snob when The Fabulous Five were in Mark Twain Elementary, but Taffy had changed a little since they'd started junior high. Now she sounded like her old self. It was probably because she had recently starred in a Hollywood movie that would be shown on television in a few months.

"I wonder if twirling a baton would be a good idea," mused Kaci Davis, a ninth-grader.

"Maybe you can twirl a television set instead," Shawnie Pendergast said sarcastically. Kaci looked down her nose at Shawnie, and a lot of kids laughed.

"I have a *super* idea," said Dekeisha. The tall black girl smiled mysteriously. "But I'm going to keep it a secret for now."

Geena McNatt's brothers, Max and Joe, stopped to see what was going on. Max was in the ninth grade and a member of the football team, and Joe was an eighth-grader.

After he read the notice, Max grumbled, "They're

really going ahead with this turnoff thing, huh? Well, there's no way I'm going to miss wrestling on TV for anybody."

"Me, either," said Joe.

"Wrestling?" asked Kaci with a sneer.

Max glared at her as the McNatt brothers moved on down the hall.

Katie was relieved to hear so many kids making plans for the assembly. That had to mean that most of them were planning to go along with the turnoff after all.

What about Tony? she wondered, thinking about how he believed she was using the turnoff to get back at him. Would he refuse to participate just to spite her?

"This TV turnoff contract says I can't watch videos or play video games," said Beth. The Fabulous Five were seated in Bumpers on Thursday afternoon after school. The turnoff contracts had been handed out just before the dismissal bell, and students had been instructed to take them home and discuss them with their families. If they decided to take part in the turnoff, they were to sign the contracts and bring them to the assembly the next day.

"They all say that," said Jana. "See, my contract is

just like yours." Jana pushed a sheet of paper toward Beth. On it was written:

I, ———————————————— *,*
AGREE TO THE FOLLOWING:
  1. *I will not watch television or videos or play any video games for two weeks.*
  2. *I will find other things to do by myself, and with my family and friends.*
  3. *I will keep a detailed diary during the turn-off that describes the things my family did together, the things I did with my friends, and everything else I did that I would not have done if I had been watching television.*
  4. *I will keep an honest record of the times when I couldn't resist and watched TV or a video or played a video game. I will also record my feelings about not watching TV.*
This contract will be for the period of —————— *through* —————— *. Upon completion of the turnoff I will receive a special award.*
  Signature ————————————————

"So if I sign this," Beth said, frowning, "I definitely can't watch the tapes the Media Club is producing, right?"

"It includes *all* videos," replied Katie.

Beth sank back against the booth and sighed. "But why does the turnoff have to happen now, just when I have my big interview with Jack Albright? How can I stand not watching that?"

Christie smiled sympathetically. "I know it will be tough, but it's just for two weeks."

"But it's the biggest interview of my life." Beth pretended to sob. "What if some big producer from a national network sees it and wants to offer me a job? How can I tell him that I haven't seen my own performance?" She sighed loudly and added, "Of course I know that won't happen. And of course I'll sign the contract. The Fabulous Five stick together, right?"

Melanie turned to Beth. "If you can wait to see your interview, I guess I can give up my soaps for two weeks."

"Thanks, guys," said Katie. "You don't know how much this means to me. Not that I'm crazy about this turnoff, either."

"Believe me, I thought long and hard about doing it," Melanie said sadly, "especially since Sylvia was run over by a motorcycle while she was shopping for her wedding dress and ended up in the hospital."

"Sylvia?" echoed Christie.

Melanie nodded. "Don't you remember her? She's

this beautiful girl on *Interns and Lovers*. She's been trying for months to get this gorgeous guy, Cal, to notice her. She's so crazy about him that she's secretly looking for a wedding dress."

"That's gross," said Katie. "Doesn't she have any other ambitions?"

Melanie shrugged. "Cal is totally gorgeous, and that's all she can think about."

"So she's in the hospital, and everything is ruined for her?" asked Jana.

"Oh, no. It's great that she had the accident!" exclaimed Melanie.

"It is?" the other four asked in unison.

"Yes. You see, Cal is an intern at the hospital. He'll have to notice her now."

"Oh, no." Katie slapped her forehead. "I can't believe this."

"Things like that can happen in real life," Melanie said defensively.

"I didn't mean I didn't believe that it could happen," said Katie. "I meant I couldn't believe anyone would watch that stuff."

Melanie stuck out her lower lip. "No matter what you think, *Interns and Lovers* is very realistic. It deals with real emotions, and the stories are sensitive and romantic. *I* think it's great."

Katie chuckled. "Okay, I give up," she said. "After hearing all that, I'm twice as glad that you're going to sign your contract."

Melanie beamed back at Katie. "The part in the contract about keeping a diary just gave me a great idea. Every afternoon when I get home from school I'm going to write down what I think is happening on *Interns and Lovers* that day. That way, I won't miss the program as much, and I can compare what I thought would happen with what really did happen after the turnoff is over."

"Hey, that's a neat idea, Mel," said Christie. "And if you predict exactly what happens, you won't have to waste time watching anymore."

At that moment, Shane, Randy, Keith, and Jon approached The Fabulous Five's booth.

"Boy, Katie, you did it to us this time," said Shane. "This contract says no video games." He waved the paper in the air. "That wipes out our Video Game Club."

"Yeah," agreed Keith, "and I was going for the championship of the club this weekend. Now it'll be two whole weeks before Jon and I can play our big match."

"You guys didn't *have* to sign it," said Katie defensively. Then she smiled and added, "But I'm glad you did."

"Since we can't play video games Saturday, like we usually do, we decided to build rockets instead," said Shane. "We're going to use the vacant lot by my house to launch them from."

"Yeah," said Jon, "and we're trying to talk Shane into letting Igor be our first astronaut."

"I think you should call him an *iguananaut*," offered Melanie.

Shane chuckled. "That's a good idea, but I don't know if he'll agree to it. He's interested in designing rockets. I think he wants to be a rocket scientist."

Suddenly a thought occurred to Katie. "Did all of you guys sign contracts?" she asked, glancing at Tony, who was across the room, talking with Bill Soliday.

Randy shrugged, and the boys looked at each other. "The four of us did," said Randy.

Katie wanted to ask about Tony, but she didn't want to look too interested. Who cares whether he signed, anyway? she asked herself. But deep down in her heart she knew that she did care—a lot.

CHAPTER

7

*F*riday afternoon Katie craned her neck to spot her friends among the kids pouring into the auditorium for the TV turnoff assembly. She wished that she could sit with them, but Mr. Bell had asked her to take part in the ceremony—had actually insisted she take part. That meant she had to sit in the back of the auditorium with the others who would be going on stage.

"Katie!" called Christie. She was waving over the heads of a group of eighth-grade girls. Katie motioned her and Jana over and then explained that she couldn't sit with them because of her part in the assembly.

"Luck," said Jana, holding up both hands for Katie to see. She had her fingers crossed on both hands.

"We'll sit down in front where you can see us while you're onstage," Christie told her. "Melanie and Beth are backstage with the other cheerleaders."

Katie watched as the two girls found seats together in the third row and squeezed in. The Fantastic Foursome were sitting in the row behind them. Katie was surprised to see Laura and Tammy. Both of them were cheerleaders and should have been backstage with the others. They're probably boycotting the turnoff, thought Katie.

Suddenly the lights in the auditorium dimmed, and the audience hushed. Over the loudspeakers came the DUM-DUM-DA-DUM of funeral music. Onstage the curtains opened ever so slowly, revealing a television set sitting on a pedestal with a funeral wreath on it. Its screen glowed white, but there was no picture. A single spotlight shone down on it.

Mr. Bell walked out onto the stage wearing a black suit. He looked very solemn as he stepped to the podium and looked out over the audience.

"Dearly beloved," he said in a hushed voice, "we are gathered here today to put an old friend to rest." He indicated the TV with a gesture of his hand. Laughter rippled through the audience.

"In keeping with this solemn occasion," he continued, "we have elected to celebrate its passing with skits, recitations, cheers, and variety acts."

Katie looked around at the kids in the audience. He had them interested. She crossed her fingers.

"For our first act, let me introduce to you Wakeman's own, Dekeisha *Cosby*."

Katie couldn't believe her eyes as Dekeisha Adams sauntered onto the stage. She was wearing long pants and a sweatshirt and had an unlit cigar in her hand and a silly smile on her face.

Oh, my gosh. She's supposed to be Bill Cosby, thought Katie.

The audience knew what she was doing right away and responded with laughter.

"Hello, ladies and gentlemen," Dekeisha said. "Oops! Sorry, I've got the wrong audience. I thought I was at Branford Junior High."

Dekeisha's act was all about how great Branford was, but everything she said could be taken as an insult instead of a compliment. When she was finished she stuck the cigar in her mouth and walked off to a standing ovation.

Curtis Trowbridge was next. He had put on a fake beard and top hat and looked like a miniature Abraham Lincoln. He read a revised version of the Emancipation

Proclamation in which he declared that all *television watchers* were being freed. Katie saw Jana and Christie nod their approval as the audience clapped for Curtis's performance.

Kaci Davis twirled her baton, and then the seventh-grade cheerleaders came on with special cheers about turning off the TV. After them came two more acts, each with a different message about why the TV should be turned off.

"Before our final act," Mr. Bell said, "I want to instruct you to *remember Branford Junior High!*"

The crowd booed and jeered at the mention of the rival school, but then everyone quieted down as the funeral music came over the loudspeakers again. Mr. Bell gave a signal, and a boy and a girl from each grade rose from their seats at the back of the auditorium. They were all wearing black, and they walked slowly onto the stage and behind the curtain. Katie followed them onto the stage and stood near the television set. She was too embarrassed to look at the audience. She hoped no one thought it was *her* idea to be in the ceremony.

When the group of boys and girls emerged from behind the curtain a moment later, they were carrying a small wooden coffin that was painted black, and they marched straight to the television set and stopped. Mr.

Bell nodded to Katie, and she reached up and pulled the plug on the TV. The glowing screen went black. There was a moment of silence before Mr. Bell lifted the set into the coffin and closed the lid, laying the wreath on top.

Mr. Bell spoke again. "As you leave the auditorium, please file past the coffin to pay your last respects to the deceased. Those of you—both students and faculty—who have signed a contract for the turnoff are asked to drop your contract into the coffin as you pass by."

The six pallbearers slowly carried the casket off the stage and down the aisle to the back of the auditorium with the principal and Katie following.

When the procession reached the back of the room, the pallbearers set the coffin down and opened the lid again, standing at attention as the last strains of funeral music died away.

The audience was quiet for a moment, and Katie couldn't tell whether they liked the idea of burying the television or not. Then, all over the auditorium, kids began jumping to their feet, applauding and cheering.

A thrill of excitement raced up Katie's back as she looked around at the cheering crowd. It would be okay. It was going to work! Most of the kids would drop signed turnoff contracts into the coffin. She just knew it.

* * *

After school The Fabulous Five crowded into Bumpers, where everybody was talking about the assembly that had officially started the turnoff.

"I have to tell you, Katie, you're a natural actress," joked Beth. "I've never seen anyone pull a plug as well as you did today."

Katie rolled her eyes. Then she laughed and asked, "Do you think Hollywood will be after me?"

Everyone at the table nodded.

"Oh, there's Dekeisha," said Beth. "I've got to tell her how good her Cosby act was. Hey, Dekeisha!"

Dekeisha heard her and headed for The Fabulous Five's table. "Hi, guys!"

"You were fantastic today!" said Beth. "I didn't know you could do imitations like that."

Dekeisha smiled shyly. "I can only do a few. Bill Cosby's my favorite. I watch his show all the time . . . or I did until I signed my TV turnoff contract." Then her smile faded. "Hey, I want to tell you, Katie, you've got trouble."

"Trouble?" asked Katie, puzzled.

"Yep. Laura McCall and her friends hung around the back of the auditorium watching everybody file past the coffin. Then they started pulling kids aside and trying to talk them into breaking their contracts."

"What?" said Katie. "You've got to be kidding."

Dekeisha shook her head. "No, I'm not. Laura's started a big campaign. She says it's a free country, and no one should dictate what you can or can't watch. I know that's what she was saying because I'm one of the kids she said it to."

"Nobody will listen to her," Katie grumbled. "At least nobody who has already decided to go along with the turnoff and has signed a contract."

"Don't bet on it," warned Dekeisha. "She's reminding everybody Mr. Bell made it clear that turning off your TV is voluntary."

Katie frowned. Maybe Laura McCall was going to be more trouble than she had thought.

CHAPTER

8

"*I still* can't believe it," said Christie. "Laura is just being spiteful."

It was the next day, and The Fabulous Five were having a meeting in Jana's bedroom. Christie and Beth were stretched across Jana's bed, sharing a bag of potato chips; Melanie was lounging on the floor, holding Jana's stuffed pink bunny; and Katie and Jana were sitting in chairs. They were all wearing their Fabulous Five T-shirts.

"You'd think since the school is behind the turnoff, she wouldn't take a chance," said Melanie.

Jana shrugged. "Like Laura said, it's strictly voluntary. I know several kids who said they weren't going to sign up. They just don't want to give up their television."

"And let's face it, even some who signed contracts won't be able to stand it without their tube time," said Beth. "They'll go berserk after the first day."

"And good old Laura will be right there to tell them it's okay to turn their sets back on," added Katie.

"We definitely have to keep as many kids from falling into her trap as we can," declared Jana.

"Mr. Bell told Mom that eighty-five percent of the student body signed up, and all of the teachers. But guess what?" Katie said, giggling. "He said he wouldn't be surprised if a couple of teachers cheated."

"I hope they get caught!" exclaimed Melanie.

"He also said that Miss Simone made photocopies of all the contracts and mailed them to the principal at Branford Junior High. Now the Branford kids will know how serious we are about beating them," continued Katie.

"I just hope Wakeman stays serious," said Jana.

"Who watched TV last night?" asked Christie.

"Not me," answered Beth.

"Me, either," said Melanie. "But it wasn't because I didn't want to." She hugged the pink bunny and looked forlornly at her friends. "Actually, it was awful.

I kept walking by the television set, and—I know you'll think I've flipped out—but I could almost hear it calling to me."

"Gosh, Mel. I didn't think you were that hooked," said Beth.

"I thought you were going to start writing your own version of the story in your diary," added Katie.

Melanie nodded. "I did, and I'll have to admit that it helped a little. In this first episode, I have Sylvia waking up in her hospital room to find Cal looking down at her. I can't wait to write another episode this afternoon."

"Boy, are Brittany and Brian grouches," said Beth. "They really hate it that we can't watch TV at our house. I'm lucky my mom and dad are all for it, or I'd be surrounded by television. That would make it hard to resist."

"Tell me about it," grumbled Melanie. "Jeffy doesn't understand why he can't watch his favorite cartoons. It's really tough on my mom to keep him entertained."

"The same with Alicia," said Beth.

"My mom and I played Monopoly last night," Katie told them. "Of course we don't watch much television, anyway."

"I went bowling with my mom and Pink," said Jana. "I kept score for them."

"So far, so good, for the five of us," said Katie. "But what are we going to do to keep Laura from luring other kids into breaking their contracts?"

"We can spread the word about what she's trying to do," said Beth. "That ought to help."

"Not everyone feels the same about Laura as we do," pointed out Jana.

"And some kids just signed up for the turnoff because everyone else was doing it," offered Christie.

"Maybe we can find out who's about to break their contracts and help them," said Katie. "When we know who they are, we can give them some ideas for fun things to do. We need to encourage them to tough it out."

"What we need to do is follow The Fantastic Foursome around and watch who they talk to," said Melanie. "Then we can corner those people and talk them back into keeping their TVs turned off."

"We can't be with The Fantastic Foursome all the time," said Christie. "We're not even in all their classes."

"What we need are spies!" Beth said dramatically.

"We've got lots of friends," said Katie. "I bet if we

talk to Dekeisha, Melinda, Mandy, and Alexis, they'll help."

"Right," agreed Christie.

The idea made Katie brim with excitement. "Let's call them right now, and see if they'll be our spies."

The Fabulous Five went to Jana's living room and took turns calling the other girls. Every one of them agreed to help. Katie felt relieved. With help, they had a fighting chance to keep Laura from ruining the turn-off.

Katie was so anxious to hear what people were saying about the turnoff on Monday morning that she gulped down her breakfast and hurried out the door. When she arrived at school, the first thing she saw was Laura taking to Shane. Oh, no, she thought. Melanie would be furious.

Intending to eavesdrop on their conversation, Katie moved closer, but just then she heard someone call her name.

"Katie Shannon. Whose big idea was this turnoff, anyway?"

Katie glanced around to see Elizabeth Harvey

marching toward her. It was obvious from her scowling face that she wasn't happy.

"I don't know why I signed up for it in the first place," Elizabeth said, stopping next to Katie. "Do you realize how long a weekend is when you can't watch TV?"

Katie smiled weakly. "Oh, come on, Elizabeth. There are lots of fun things to do besides watch television."

"Name one," Elizabeth challenged.

By this time Lisa Snow had joined them. "Yeah," she said. "This was the longest weekend of my life. I'll never last two whole weeks."

"Sure you will," Katie insisted.

"Well, I won't," said Elizabeth. "And you were going to name something fun to do besides watch TV, remember?"

Katie nodded. "Listen, guys. Don't give up yet. Just give it a little time. You'll think of things to do."

Elizabeth shrugged and walked away, calling back over her shoulder, "If I don't think of something pretty quickly, I'm going straight home to turn on my set."

"I signed up for the turnoff, and I'd still like to do it," said Lisa, "but my family isn't interested. My dad wants to watch the news when he gets home, and then if there's a game on later, he wants to watch that. My mom has some shows in the evening that she says she *has* to watch. I either have to sit in my room by myself or be in the living room with them. I might as well forget about the whole thing now and get it over with."

"Can't you explain to your parents how important the TV turnoff is?" asked Katie. "Didn't you tell them the whole school is doing it?"

"That's not true. Laura was telling me about all the kids who aren't going along with it."

"There are more doing it than not," argued Katie. "What about Branford? Do you want them to beat Wakeman? Think of how they'll make fun of us, after we said we could do better than them."

"I know," Lisa said, sounding miserable. "But I can't get away from TV, anyway, so why fight it?"

Now what am I going to do? thought Katie as she left Lisa and scuffed along toward The Fabulous Five's meeting place by the fence.

She glanced around to see Melissa McConnell and Tammy Lucero talking to Marcie Bee near the gum tree, where the Wakeman kids stuck their gum before going into school. Katie watched them for a moment, and even though she couldn't hear what they were saying, she knew what they were talking about. Marcie had signed a contract to give up TV.

Jana and Christie were waiting when Katie got to the fence.

"I've got good news," announced Jana.

"Great," replied Katie. "I could use some."

"I talked to Randy," Jana went on. "He said the guys made rockets at his house on Saturday and launched them yesterday. They had a great time. The best news for you is that Tony was with them. He signed up for the turnoff, too."

Katie felt her spirits rise. "Did Randy say if Tony talked about me?" she asked.

"No, but I can ask him if you want me to," offered Jana.

"Never mind," Katie answered quickly. If he's going to be too stubborn to apologize to me, I'm certainly not going to give him the satisfaction of knowing that I care.

CHAPTER

9

"How did your weekend go, class?" asked Mrs. Clark that day. "Did any of you have trouble finding things to do instead of watching television?"

"I counted the money I've been saving for a trip to Disney World and read two books," said Melinda Thaler.

"Some of us guys made rockets," said Scott Daly. "Then I tried to see how many push-ups I could do. I got up to seventy-five."

"Very good," said Mrs. Clark.

"I wrote on my little brother's feet and stomach," bragged Joel Murphy. He looked around impishly when a chorus of laughter filled the air.

"You what?" asked Mrs. Clark, looking surprised.

"Well, actually I copied the Declaration of Independence on him. I just wanted to see if I could do it. It looked really neat."

"I'm sure it did," said the teacher, shaking her head.

"He didn't like it when I held him down, though, and he started crying. My mom got mad and turned on the television to keep him quiet."

Whitney Larkin frowned at Joel and raised her hand. "Curtis Trowbridge and I went to the library and checked out a bunch of books. We read the whole weekend."

"Very commendable," said Mrs. Clark. "What about you, Geena?"

"I wasn't crazy about the turnoff, but I signed up. Then my brothers had the television on all weekend. I tried not to watch, but it wasn't easy."

"Good for you for trying," said Mrs. Clark.

Others said they had found things to do with their friends and with their families. A few admitted to sneaking a peek at television.

Katie didn't think it sounded as if the turnoff was going too badly for some kids. At least the news was a little encouraging.

*　*　*

"I saw Laura and Tammy talking to Lisa Snow," reported Mandy. "I talked to Lisa later, and she said she was definitely considering breaking her contract." Mandy and Alexis were sitting with The Fabulous Five at Bumpers after school, giving their spy reports.

Turning to Alexis, Katie said, "What did you find out?"

"I saw Melissa talking to Mona Vaughn and Matt Zeboski," said Alexis. "I couldn't tell for sure, but I think it was about the turnoff."

"Darn," said Katie. "She's already talking some kids into watching television, and this is just the beginning of the first week. By the end of next week she may have everyone breaking the contract, and then the whole turnoff will fall apart."

"Hey, guys. Listen to this," cried Dekeisha as she pushed her way through the crowd and sank breathlessly into The Fabulous Five's booth. "You'll never guess what The Fantastic Foursome is up to now."

"What?" asked Christie.

Dekeisha caught her breath and leaned forward. "Laura and her friends are saying that they'll watch programs for anybody who'll pay them fifty cents an hour. They say that they'll write down everything that happens on the show and bring the report to school the next day."

"That's cheating," Katie blurted out. "That way kids could keep their contracts and still know what's happening on their favorite shows right away instead of waiting to see the tapes they've made on their VCRs."

"Exactly," said Dekeisha. "That's what Laura is counting on."

"Right." Jana nodded. "And I'll bet she's also planning to secretly let Mr. Bell know who is cheating."

"And if she gets enough kids to cheat, the turnoff will be a failure," said Dekeisha.

"That jerk," said Katie. "I just hope nobody takes her up on it."

"Ha!" scoffed Dekeisha. "That's the rest of the news. She was passing around a sign-up sheet in science class, and half the kids in class were signing up."

Katie sank back against the booth, folding her arms across her chest. It made her furious that Laura was trying so hard to wreck the turnoff. But it made her even angrier that so many kids were going along with it.

The crowd in Bumpers began to thin. Dekeisha left with Mandy and Alexis, leaving The Fabulous Five alone with their gloom.

Suddenly, Jana sat up straight. "Don't look now, but you-know-who is coming this way."

Katie turned to see The Fantastic Foursome approaching.

"Well, how's the great reformer?" Laura asked in a sarcastic voice. She was looking straight at Katie. "Have you come up with any more great ideas like the TV turnoff? I hear there are lots of kids who aren't going along with it."

"Only because you and your friends are trying to talk people into watching television," said Katie.

"That's not totally true," replied Laura sweetly. "A lot of them only went along with the turnoff in the first place because your mother got Mr. Bell to make such a big deal of it. Who cares if the Branford kids didn't watch TV? Big deal."

"Well, it *is* a big deal to beat Branford," said Beth defensively.

"I also heard that you're trying something really low and sneaky to get kids to cheat on their contracts. You'll never get away with it."

Laura ignored Katie. Instead she turned to Melanie. "I hear you like to watch *Interns and Lovers*, Melanie. Did you watch it Friday after school?"

"Of course not!" said Melanie proudly.

"Then you probably don't know that Sylvia almost died, do you?" asked Laura.

"She did?" Laura had Melanie's complete attention.

"Yes, she did. Cal and the other doctors did everything they could to save her. I can't tell you how dramatic it was. It looks as if she's *really* going to die this time. She's unconscious again. When the show ended, Cal was sitting next to Sylvia's bed holding her hand, and tears were running down his cheeks."

"Wow! Poor Cal," whispered Melanie.

"I know you signed a contract to turn off your TV," Laura said.

She was looking at Melanie sympathetically, and to Katie's horror, Melanie was looking back at her, misery showing plainly in her eyes.

"Why don't you let me watch my tape of *Interns and Lovers* for you this evening?" Laura asked. "I'm going to, anyway. I can't stand to wait another day to find out if she regains consciousness. I'll call you afterward and tell you what happened. It will only cost you fifty cents."

Melanie glared at Laura. "*That's a dirty trick, Laura McCall!* No, I will not pay you to watch *Interns and Lovers*. Nothing you can say will make me cheat."

"Suit yourself." Laura flashed a sly grin. "But stay tuned. I may give you an update on how Sylvia's doing, anyway. And then again . . . maybe I won't," she said with a confident look. She raised an eyebrow at Katie.

"You'd better stay tuned, too, Katie Shannon." With a flip of her braid, Laura walked off.

Katie couldn't get Laura off her mind all evening. No matter how hard she tried to concentrate on her homework, she kept thinking of The Fantastic Foursome and their trick to get people to cheat.

Midway through the evening Willie knocked on Katie's door. "Can I come in?"

"Sure, Mom."

"How's the turnoff going?" asked Willie.

Katie shrugged. "Okay, I guess."

"Come on. Tell me what you really think, sweetheart," Willie insisted. "To hear Mr. Bell tell it, it couldn't be more perfect, but I know better than that. What's going on in the trenches?"

Katie smiled at her mother. "There are some problems," she admitted. "For one thing, Laura McCall is trying to get kids to cheat on their contracts by offering to watch TV for them if they pay her."

"She is!" said Willie in amazement. "Why?"

Katie hesitated. "Mostly because I'm for the turnoff, and . . . because you're helping Mr. Bell with it, and you're my mother."

Willie sat quietly for a moment. Then she reached

out and put her arm around Katie. "I'm sorry, honey. I wish I could do something to help. There are always going to be people in the world we can't get along with, I guess. Sometimes there's no explaining why."

"I know." Katie sounded dejected. "And another thing, Lisa Snow told me that she was having trouble sticking with the turnoff at home because her parents like to watch television. Her father doesn't want to give up his news, and her mother has programs she doesn't want to miss, either. And Lisa's not the only one with that problem. Some of the kids with little brothers and sisters say their parents won't turn off the cartoon shows because it keeps the kids entertained."

"That's *exactly* the problem with television!" Willie said angrily. "Parents stick their kids in front of the TV because it's easier than helping them find constructive things to do. Things that will teach them to think. Now *that's* something I can do something about!"

Willie marched to the door with her hands on her hips. "I've got another article to write."

CHAPTER

10

"You should have tasted the double-fudge chocolate cake I made last night instead of watching TV, Katie," said Melinda Thaler. Katie was standing by the fence with a group of girls the next morning waiting for school to start. "It was absolutely colossal. I think I may become a gourmet cook. Tonight I'm going to dig through all my mother's cookbooks and copy down the best-sounding recipes."

"Well, I started something I've always wanted to do," said Heather Clark. "I'm writing a book. It's really going to be great. It's about this thirteen-year-old girl whose name is Heidi Clay. She's simply gorgeous, and she goes to this school called Wakefield Junior High. All the boys in her school are madly in love with her."

"The names sound just a little bit familiar," laughed Marcie Bee. "Heidi Clay and Heather Clark. Wakefield Junior High and Wakeman Junior High. Shouldn't you change them more to protect the guilty?"

"I couldn't find *anything* to do," complained Sara Sawyer. "I was bored out of my gourd."

"Did you try getting your family to play some kind of game?" asked Katie. "Like Pictionary or Monopoly?"

Sara shook her head. "I tried, but no one was interested. My dad worked on an antique car he's had sitting in the garage for ages, and my mother decided to take up quilting. My brothers played basketball most of the time. Instead of our doing things together, we were doing them separately."

"There's nothing wrong with that," said Christie. "You just have to find something to do that interests you."

"But I don't like to cook or write like Melinda and Heather do."

"What about reading or organizing your room?" asked Jana. "I've got my room in such good shape, my mother didn't recognize it."

"I don't like to read, and I consider cleaning my room *punishment*," Sara said, folding her arms across her chest.

"I'm having trouble finding things to do, too," said Mona Vaughn.

A warning signal flashed through Katie's brain. More and more of her friends were getting discouraged with the turnoff. Now that Laura was offering to help kids cheat, pretty soon the TV turnoff would be a complete failure. Katie could just imagine Laura and her friends laughing at Katie and her mother.

She worried about it all day and set aside her homework that evening to make a list of things her classmates could do instead of watching TV.

1. *Talk on the phone with your friends.*

That should interest lots of girls, but their parents will probably throw a fit, she thought, and chuckled.

2. *Tie-dye a T-shirt or anything made of cotton, even a pair of socks.*
3. *Decorate a pair of sneakers with paint, glitter glue, or beads.*
4. *Get your friends together and make each other friendship bracelets woven with embroidery thread.*

   5. *Snap pictures of your friends. Take some goofy shots and some serious ones, then make a collage of your favorites to hang on your bedroom wall.*

   6. *Borrow your parents' camcorder and make a movie starring your friends. Of course you won't be able to watch it until the turnoff is over.*

Katie glanced down at her list, surprised at how fast it was growing. Still, there was something missing. She read the list again and realized that every activity she had thought of so far would appeal mostly to girls. She hadn't thought of a single thing especially for boys to do. Of course there were sports, but there had to be more than that.

She was still thinking this over when she heard the phone ring.

"Katie," Willie called from downstairs. "It's Jana."

Katie hurried downstairs and picked up the phone. "Hi, Jana. What's up?"

"Trouble," said Jana. "You're not going to believe this, but I just talked to Randy, and he said that Laura McCall is having a party Saturday night. A *television* party!"

"What?" exclaimed Katie. "What do you mean, a television party?"

"According to Randy, Laura is telling everybody that her dad is going to put three or four television sets in their living room and family room, and she's going to have tons of food and soda, plus video games."

Katie was too stunned to speak for a moment. This was bound to mean the end of the turnoff. Too many kids were threatening to break their contracts anyway, and a big party at Laura's would be the only excuse they needed.

"How did Randy find out about it?" asked Katie. "Did Laura invite him?"

"You bet she did," Jana answered angrily. "She and her friends have been on the phone all evening calling kids and inviting them to her party. Randy told her he wouldn't go."

"They wouldn't have the nerve to call any of The Fabulous Five," said Katie.

"No, just our boyfriends," said Jana.

Katie winced. There was no doubt that Laura would invite Tony. But would he go?

"We're going to have to talk to all the people we can in the morning," Jana continued, "and try to keep them from going to Laura's party."

"Right," said Katie, sounding more confident than she felt.

*   *   *

The next morning Katie hurried into the building the moment she got to school and posted her list on the bulletin board. Outside again she saw Jana talking to Mona just inside the Wakeman fence. Katie stopped a few feet away and waited until they finished their conversation. Then she hurried over to Jana. "What did she say? Did Laura invite her to the party?"

Jana nodded. "She asked Mona and Matt both. Mona doesn't want to, but Matt does. He thinks having four television sets going at once would be a ball. Mona said she's sorry, but if she can't talk Matt out of going, she's going, too."

"Great," Katie muttered.

The rest of The Fabulous Five were already waiting at their meeting spot, and they had all heard about Laura's party.

"What are we going to do?" asked Melanie. "We can't let her get away with this."

"I don't know," confessed Katie. "She's going to be hard to stop this time."

"*Everybody's* talking about Laura's party," said Christie, sliding her hot-lunch tray onto the table and sitting down beside Jana in the cafeteria at noon.

"I know," said Melanie. "Brian Olsen must have told me four times that he's going."

"Is Shane going?" Beth asked Melanie.

She shrugged. "I haven't talked to him today."

"Now's your chance," said Jana. "He's over by the steam tables talking with Keith. Maybe you can find out if Laura has asked him."

"Good idea," said Melanie, jumping up and heading in his direction.

She was back in a couple of minutes, smiling broadly. "Shane isn't going to Laura's party. He wants to be one of the people who goes the whole two weeks without watching television. He says he loves the challenge."

"Did Keith say anything about the party?" asked Beth.

Melanie shook her head.

Katie glanced at Tony. He had finished his lunch and was heading out the cafeteria door. She was positive now that Laura would invite him, if she hadn't already. And she was almost as positive that he would go because he was mad at her. Just then a horrible thought occurred to her. Maybe that was what Laura had meant at Bumpers when she had told Katie to "stay tuned." Maybe Tony had already said yes.

She sighed and turned her attention back to her friends.

"You look great today, Beth," Jana was saying. "But aren't you a little dressed up for school? That's the outfit you wore for the first Media Club broadcast, isn't it?"

Beth nodded. "Today is my interview with Jack Albright. Mr. Levine is taking the Media Club down to the television station for the taping right after school. Jon Smith gets to operate the camera, and Tim Riggs is going to be the director. The rest of the club members are going to help out however they can."

"Lucky you," said Melanie. "I watch Jack Albright on *Taking Chances* all the time. Whoops!" she said, gulping back a giggle. "I meant I *used* to watch it all the time. Before the turnoff."

"I am lucky," agreed Beth, "but it's torture for me not to be able to see the tape of the interview for a week and a half. I don't know about this turnoff," she added, looking dejected.

Katie nodded sympathetically, trying to give Beth some extra encouragement.

Jana looked puzzled. "What I don't understand is why the Media Club is going ahead with its Saturday morning cable TV show if nobody's supposed to watch

TV? Why doesn't the club just wait to broadcast the show after the turnoff is over?"

"Don't forget," said Beth. "The turnoff is voluntary. Some kids will watch the show, and how could we ever reschedule an interview with a superstar? Besides, Mr. Levine said that we'd lose our Saturday morning slot with the cable station if we didn't produce shows for two weeks."

Gloom hung over the table for a few minutes until Jana asked, "How's your diary coming, Melanie? Have you come up with any more episodes for *Interns and Lovers*?"

Melanie's face brightened. "Oh, yes! Now that Sylvia has regained consciousness, she has to learn to walk all over again. And guess who's helping her?"

"Don't tell us. Let us guess," said Christie, winking at the others. "Could it possibly be Cal?"

Melanie gave Christie a disgusted look. "Of course it's Cal. And when he held her for the first time and guided her down the hospital corridor, he promised her that as soon as she was well again, he'd take her back to the amusement park where they met. It was so romantic that I cried."

"I don't know why you bother to watch soaps when you can write your own," said Katie.

"I love doing it," Melanie admitted. "I wonder how close I'll be to what's happening on the show."

Suddenly Katie sat upright. "I think I may have an idea about how to keep kids from Laura's party," she said. "What do you think about trying to get a bunch of kids to take a bike ride Saturday to the amusement park? Melanie's soap opera story gave me the idea. We could bike out to Adventureland in the afternoon and get everyone to meet later at Mama Mia's for pizza."

"That's not bad," said Beth, nodding thoughtfully. "As a matter of fact, I think it's a very good idea."

"I'll bet a lot of kids would like to go," Jana agreed.

"And if they went to Adventureland and then to Mama Mia's, there wouldn't be time to go to Laura's party," Christie said gleefully. "We could ask people like Lisa and Mona and Matt and Brian."

"And Shelly Bramlett and Geena McNatt," said Jana.

"And the boys who like to watch baseball," added Katie. "We've got to ask them."

"What you really mean is we need to ask Tony, don't you, Katie?" Jana asked gently.

Katie sighed and nodded. She missed Tony a lot.

"I'll talk to Randy about going to the park," said Jana. "I'll hint to him that it would be nice if he'd ask Tony to come, too."

"Do you think he'll come?" asked Katie. "You said Tony was really mad at me."

Jana shrugged. "All we can do is try."

"I'll talk to Keith," said Beth. "Maybe if all the other guys are going, Tony will want to go, too."

"And I'll talk to Shane," offered Melanie.

"Thanks," said Katie. "You guys are super friends."

"We're The Fabulous Five," said Jana, grabbing her friend's hand and squeezing it.

CHAPTER

11

*T*hat afternoon Katie talked to Mona Vaughn and Lisa Snow about the bike ride to Adventureland. At first Mona was interested, but Lisa seemed indifferent.

"It's going to be so much fun," insisted Katie. "And we're asking tons of kids to come, like Bill Soliday and Tony Sanchez."

Lisa immediately perked up. "You're asking Bill? Did he say he was going?"

"I'm sure he will," fibbed Katie. She knew Lisa had a crush on Bill. "After all, all his friends will be there."

"Oh," said Lisa. "Well, if Bill's going, you can count me in."

"Great," said Katie. "We're going to leave from the school at one-thirty."

"I don't know if Matt will want to go to Mama Mia's afterward, though," said Mona. "He's awfully interested in going to Laura's party."

"You can talk him into it, Mona," replied Katie. "I know you can."

Katie saw Bill and Scott standing next to the Wurlitzer jukebox in Bumpers after school. She hurried over to talk to them.

"Did you guys hear about the bike trip to Adventureland on Saturday?" she asked.

"Yeah, and it sounds great, Katie," said Bill. "Count us in."

"Will you go to Mama Mia's for pizza later?"

Bill and Scott glanced at each other.

"Well, we, uh . . . we kind of had something else we wanted to do then," said Scott.

Katie narrowed her eyes. "You're not going to Laura's to watch TV, are you? What about your turn-off contract?"

Scott looked at Bill, who looked down at his shoes. "Er, we were thinking about going to her party."

"But what about Branford Junior High?" Katie demanded. "If you watch television, you'll hurt our chances of beating them."

"It wouldn't be like losing a football or basketball game," insisted Scott.

"Yeah," agreed Bill. "It's just watching TV."

"Fine," Katie snapped, turning on her heel. She was furious, but if the boys wanted to break their contracts, there wasn't much she could do about it.

As Katie spun around, she bumped right into Tony Calcaterra. She was speechless as they stared into each other's eyes for what seemed like ages. Finally she pulled her gaze away from his and stormed back to where Christie, Jana, and Melanie were standing.

"Wow! That was some article your mother wrote for today's paper," Beth said the next morning as she opened her locker. "She really cut down parents who aren't helping their kids with the TV turnoff."

Katie groaned. "As if one article wasn't enough, she had to write two.

"By the way," she asked Beth, "how'd your interview with Jack Albright go?"

Beth's eyes lit up. "Super. He was really nice, and totally gorgeous. He autographed my purse for me, right on the front, where everyone can see it. I've decided I'll survive not watching the tape until the week after next. Every time I close my eyes, I see his face as clear as TV, anyway!" She sighed dreamily.

"Are you surviving not watching your soaps, Mel?" asked Katie. "You haven't been cheating, have you?"

"Who, me, cheat?" Melanie raised her eyebrows in a show of innocence. "I certainly have not."

"Tell us about the latest episode of *Interns and Lovers* you've written, Mel," said Christie.

"I'm glad you asked," said Melanie, digging into her purse and pulling out a small spiral notebook. "The way I've got it figured out, see, is that Sylvia's convalescing now and Cal is spending all his time at the hospital with her. He doesn't realize it yet, but he's falling in love."

"Something told me it would turn out that way," said Christie with a smile.

"Katie," Mrs. Karl called, as the study period came to an end. "Would you drop this envelope off at the office for me?"

"Yes, ma'am."

As Katie hurried along the busy hallway, she saw Tony walking ahead of her with Bill and Scott. She felt a tug at her heart as the three boys laughed and jostled each other. Part of her wanted to tell Tony she missed him, but another part of her still felt that he was the one who owed her the apology. It was obvious that he was still angry at her, too.

When Katie entered the office, Miss Simone was at her desk, looking totally frazzled.

Mr. Bell was standing nearby with an exasperated look on his face.

"Miss Simone, that was at least the tenth irate call I've gotten about the article in this morning's paper. Please take my calls from now on."

Then, noticing Katie, he frowned. "Oh, hello, Katie. I didn't see you standing there." He turned and went back into his office.

"Mrs. Karl asked me to give you this envelope, Miss Simone," said Katie.

"Thank you, dear."

Katie hesitated before leaving. "Miss Simone, was Mr. Bell talking about my mother's article that was in the paper this morning?"

The secretary looked at Katie and smiled. "I'm afraid he was. It's part of his job to take flak, and he doesn't really mind it this time. He knows it's for a good cause."

"Why is he getting so many angry calls?" asked Katie.

"Some of the parents feel that the article was directed at them," Miss Simone replied, "and they think the school may have talked your mother into writing it. I think there are a few guilty consciences out there."

Boy, Katie thought as she hurried to her next class. What a mess the turnoff was shaping up to be. It had sounded so simple at first. People would turn off their televisions for two weeks and find something else to do. But things had quickly become a lot more complicated.

Katie squared her shoulders and stuck out her chin as she marched into her next class. One thing was certain—she wasn't going to give up on the TV turnoff. In spite of everything, it *was* a good idea.

CHAPTER

12

Katie looked around the crowded school yard in amazement. There were boys and girls with bicycles all over the place. Some of them, including Tony, Bill, and Scott, were seventh-graders, but there were kids from eighth and ninth grade, too. Even the McNatts were going to Adventureland. Then Katie noticed Laura McCall and her friends.

"I can't believe it," said Katie. "Laura's here. She's actually coming."

Jana shrugged. "I guess so."

"Don't worry about Laura, Katie," said Melanie. "This has turned out great. Except for sports events and dances, it's one of the first things Wacko kids have ever done together as one big group."

"Right," agreed Katie. "At least the first part of the plan is working. That doesn't mean everyone will go out for pizza together tonight, though. Laura will probably spend the whole afternoon inviting kids to her party."

"If they all went out for pizza, Mama Mia's couldn't handle them, anyway," commented Christie.

"There are a lot of other places for kids to go, like Taco Plenty and Bumpers," said Jana. "Maybe they'll want to do that instead of going to Laura's to watch TV."

"We'd better get started," said Katie grimly. She got on her bike and pushed off. *"Let's go, everybody!"* she shouted.

"Head 'em up, and move 'em out!" yelled Shane.

Katie rode out of the school yard with a stream of bicyclers behind her and headed for the amusement park.

At Adventureland, Jana, Melanie, and Beth went on rides with their boyfriends, while Katie went with Christie. She was having fun with her friend, but it felt odd not being with Tony. They usually went to places like this as a couple. Every once in a while she spotted him with Scott and Bill. Lisa was with them, too, but Katie noticed that Bill wasn't paying much attention to her.

The Wakeman students were spread out all over the park and seemed to be having a great time. Kids waved to her from every ride she passed. Well, at least the TV turnoff accomplished one thing, thought Katie. It got everyone together to have fun. Then she saw Tony standing in line to go on the super Ferris wheel. Everyone but me, that is.

But in spite of missing Tony, Katie found that the afternoon passed quickly.

"Super idea, Katie," said Daphne Alexandrou when Katie and Christie stopped at the refreshment tent to get ice cream. "We ought to do this more often."

"Yeah," chimed in Shelly Bramlett.

Katie smiled with pleasure as she and Christie found seats at the table where Jana, Melanie, and Beth were sitting with their boyfriends.

Glancing around, she saw Tony, Scott, and Bill sitting not far away. Near them were Max and Joe McNatt with some other eighth- and ninth-grade boys. They were wearing their red-and-gold Wakeman jackets. Kaci Davis and Kyle Zimmerman, another ninth-grader, were holding hands as they walked into the tent. Mona and Matt were talking nearby. Laura and her friends were there, too. The tent was full of Wakeman kids.

Just then three boys wearing black letter jackets with large red *B*'s on them walked into the tent carrying sodas. Katie watched as other Branford kids trickled into the tent after them.

Uh-oh, thought Katie. This could mean trouble, especially if the principal of Branford Junior High told his students about Wakeman's challenge. She cringed as she remembered that Miss Simone had even sent copies of Wakeman's turnoff contracts to the other school.

One of the boys wearing a Branford jacket nudged the boy standing next to him and said in a loud voice, "Hey, aren't those some of the Wakeman wimps over there?"

His friend glanced around and said, "Yeah. I think you're right. Did you hear the big joke that they think they can beat us?"

While both boys broke up laughing, some of the Wakeman students began grumbling among themselves.

"Of course we can beat you!" Max McNatt yelled.

"What are we going to do?" whispered Melanie.

"I don't know," said Katie. "But if we don't think of something, this could turn into a fight."

Suddenly Katie noticed four girls. They were cheerleaders whom she'd met after a Branford-Wakeman football game when she, Jana, and Christie had gone down to see Beth and Melanie on the field.

Katie looked at Beth. "Recognize those girls?"

"Yeah, they're Jill, Ruthie, Kristin, and Dina from the Branford squad. They're really nice."

"Hey, you're right," said Melanie. "Let's say hello."

"Well, I just had an idea," said Katie. "What do you think of this?" She bent closer and told them her idea.

"It just might work," said Beth. "Come on. Let's find out."

The Fabulous Five hurried over to the Branford cheerleaders and said hello.

After they had chatted for a few minutes, Katie said, "We had an idea we wanted to talk to you about."

"What's that?" asked Jill, the tall, dark-haired cheerleader.

"You must have heard that Wakeman is having a TV turnoff like the one Branford had," Katie continued.

"Right," said Ruthie. "Our principal told us about it. How's it going?"

"Pretty well," answered Katie. "But we thought it

would be fun if each school did cheers for the TV turnoff, just like we do at games. Maybe just a couple to stir up some excitement? Besides, if we get the crowd started having fun, it might keep fights from breaking out. Branford and Wakeman are pretty big rivals."

"Hmm," said Jill, looking thoughtful. "That might work, and it does sound like fun. What do you think?" she asked, turning to the others.

"Great," said Dina, a short blond. "Let's do it."

The other two girls nodded.

"Most of the seventh-grade cheerleaders are here, plus a few from the varsity squad," said Jill. "We'll get our cheerleaders together, and you get yours. When you're ready, let us know." The four girls ran off.

"I'll get Dekeisha and Mandy," offered Beth.

"There's Taffy," said Christie. "I'll get her."

"I'll talk to Kaci," volunteered Melanie. Then she frowned. "Laura and Melissa are cheerleaders, too. Who's going to tell them?"

"I will," said Katie firmly.

"You've got to be kidding, Katie Shannon," snapped Laura after Katie approached her with her idea. "That's the dumbest thing I ever heard of."

"Yeah. Count us out," said Melissa.

"Have it your way," replied Katie. "We just wanted to give you a chance to join in."

"What are they doing?" Katie heard kids whispering as the two groups of girls lined up on one side of the tent.

"I think they're going to do cheers," someone said.

All the Wakeman and Branford kids were craning their necks to see. Kaci Davis had taken command of the Wakeman cheerleaders, since she was the captain of the varsity squad. She nodded to Jill that they were ready.

Jill nodded back, and the Branford cheerleaders stood with their arms stretched out in front of them and their fists together. When Jill gave the signal, they began to cheer:

> We've got the spirit,
> We've got the pride.
> We've got the spirit,
> We're ridin' high.
> Go, Branford,
> Beat Wakeman.
> Show 'em how to win!

They ended the cheer with spread eagles.

All the Branford kids in the audience cheered and waved their fists in the air.

Kaci waited until they quieted and then signaled the Wakeman squad to begin their cheer.

> *Stand up, Wakeman Warriors,*
> *Stand up tall.*
> *Lookin' good, Warriors,*
> *Shout!*
> *Shout it out!*
> *Shout it out loud!*

The cheerleaders formed a low pyramid, which almost touched the ceiling of the tent.

> *We can do it,*
> *We will do it,*
> *We'll do it every time.*
> *Beat Branford,*
> *Beat Branford now!*

The Wakeman crowd went wild, hooting and yelling. But we just kept a *real* fight from breaking out, Katie thought gleefully. Everybody is having a super time.

Next the Branford cheerleaders got up again, and

the students tried to make as much noise as the Wakeman kids had. Each time one of the squads did a cheer, the noise got louder. When the Wakeman cheerleaders were up, they shouted the cheer at the Branford kids, and when the Branford kids were cheering, they shouted their yell at the Wakeman crowd. Katie even heard Max and Joe McNatt cheering with the crowd, "Go, Wakeman! Beat Branford!"

Then Katie saw Laura fuming at the back of the tent. Laura pulled her three best friends close to her and started talking to them and frowning in The Fabulous Five's direction at the same time. Uh-oh, Katie thought. Our troubles may not be over yet.

CHAPTER

13

*M*ama Mia's was bursting at the seams with Wakeman kids that evening. Four long lines were formed at the order counter, and the tables and booths were all filled. Small groups stood talking and eating slices of pizza. Katie was crammed into a booth with the rest of The Fabulous Five and with Randy, Shane, and Keith.

She looked around at the crowd. The Fabulous Five had gone by Bumpers on the way to the pizza place, and it had looked crowded, too. Katie guessed that Taco Plenty and the other fast-food restaurants were also filled. If Laura was still having her television party, there couldn't be many people there. At least she hoped not.

"Having the cheerleaders perform was a great idea, Katie," said Jana. "When I saw the looks on the Wakeman kids' faces, I knew they weren't going to let Branford beat us in the TV turnoff."

"Even the McNatts are here," said Melanie. "I never would have believed that."

"And look," Christie chimed in. "There's Tony sitting with Bill and Scott. They didn't go to Laura's party, either. Aren't you glad, Katie?"

Katie shrugged. "Maybe they got their school spirit back today."

"I don't think so," said Randy. "They decided not to go before this afternoon. Tony was all over Bill and Scott about going to Laura's party. He was unmerciful."

"*What?*" cried Katie. She couldn't believe what she was hearing.

Shane nodded. "Tony was really on their case. I haven't seen him so carried away since Mr. Bell told him he couldn't wear an earring to school."

Katie stared across the room at Tony. Were Randy and Shane telling the truth? Had Tony really been on her side all along? But why had he talked Bill and

Scott out of going to Laura's party, she wondered, when he was so angry with her?

As she was watching, Tony left his booth and went to stand in one of the food lines.

Katie jumped to her feet. "Excuse me. I need to get out."

Tony was concentrating on the list of pizzas and soft drinks and didn't notice Katie when she got in line behind him. Katie cleared her throat, but he still didn't notice, so she tugged on his sleeve.

Tony turned around, looking surprised. "Oh, Your Honor."

"Hi," Katie responded softly. "I just heard that you talked Bill and Scott out of going to Laura's party and breaking their TV turnoff contracts. Thanks."

He smiled at her, and then the two of them stood there awkwardly for a few seconds. Finally Katie took a deep breath.

"I'm sorry, I . . ." she began, just as Tony said the same thing. They stopped and looked at each other in surprise.

"I'm sorry I was so stubborn," Tony said quickly.

"That's exactly what I was going to say," said Katie. "I got angry instead of talking."

Tony smiled and took Katie's hand. "I should have

been able to see that you were upset over my watching baseball all the time, but by the time I did realize it, I thought you were organizing the turnoff to get back at me."

Katie grinned. "I did want you to stop watching TV, but that's not why I was involved in the turnoff. Actually, the turnoff was my mom's idea, and I was just as mad at her for starting it as you were at me. But when kids at school started bad-mouthing her, I had to get involved. Now I'm glad I did."

"Me, too," Tony said. There was a twinkle in his eye as he added, "Actually, since the turnoff, I've been reading about the games in the newspaper. Some of the write-ups are pretty good, and I haven't missed watching them on TV as much as I thought I would. And I've got to tell you, I've been reading all the stats, too, so now I'm really an expert on baseball."

Katie groaned. "Oh, no. Now you'll never have time for me."

Tony shook his head, looking more serious. "Yes, I will, Your Honor."

She looked up at him and squeezed his hand.

"I heard there was no one, but *no one*, at Laura's party Saturday," Beth said gleefully. The Fabulous Five were gathered at their spot by the fence on Monday morning.

"I passed her when I got to school just now, and she stuck her nose in the air," reported Jana. "She's really mad."

"Too bad," said Katie, grinning.

As they were talking, Lisa Snow ran up. "Oh, Katie," said Lisa happily, "I wanted to tell you, my parents read your mother's article about families' not helping their kids with the turnoff. Boy, were they mad at first. They started raving about all the reasons why they shouldn't quit watching. My dad said there was no way he could miss the news, and my mother said she couldn't miss her programs, either.

"But the more they talked, the more they said they could do without television if other people could. And guess what, they each started a book and couldn't put it down."

"Super," replied Katie. "I'm glad to hear it."

More and more during the rest of the week, kids came up to Katie and told her about the things they had found to do instead of watching TV. Some mentioned the list of activities she had posted on the bulletin board. Others talked about doing things with their families. Geena McNatt said that Max and Joe had talked their father into digging out their fishing equipment, and she and her father and brothers had gone fishing together. They'd had so much fun, they were planning a two-day family fishing trip.

Later that day Katie got a note saying that Miss Simone wanted to see her.

"I thought you might be worrying about the phone calls Mr. Bell was getting from people complaining about your mother's article," said the secretary. "You should know that a lot of those people have called him back to apologize. They realize now that they should have been more supportive of their children's efforts not to watch television."

Katie looked through the doorway into the principal's office. Mr. Bell was talking on the telephone and had a big smile on his face.

"Thank you, Miss Simone. That does make me feel good."

Katie held Tony's hand as she looked around the gym and watched couples dancing to the music of The Dreadful Alternatives. Crepe paper had been strung across the walls of the Wakeman gym, and there were long tables topped with soft drinks and trays of home-made cookies, brownies, and cake. The turnoff was finally over, and this was the party to celebrate its end.

She couldn't help feeling a mixture of pride and re-lief. Pride that she had helped to make it a success, even though she hadn't been for it in the beginning, and relief that things could get back to normal now. She looked across the floor to where her mother was talking with Mr. Bell and Mrs. Karl. She was proud of her mother most of all. Willie had never backed down from something she believed in, and Katie had learned a lot about standing up to pressure during the turnoff.

Jana and Randy and Melanie and Shane were stand-ing next to Katie and Tony. No one was talking. In-stead each couple swayed to the music and watched the crowd clustered around the room.

Suddenly Beth hurried toward them. She was fol-lowed by Jon Smith, who was carrying a camcorder with a light on top. Wires ran down Jon's back to a battery pack that was attached to the belt at the back of his waist.

"I'm interviewing people for the Media Club. Can I interview you guys?" Beth asked. "You'll be able to see yourselves on TV."

"You forget," Tony said with a laugh. "Katie doesn't watch TV."

"I didn't say I wouldn't like to be *on* television," joked Katie. "After all, I might have to try a famous court case when I become a judge someday, and there's bound to be publicity."

"Just think of it as a news program, which is really what it is," said Beth. "Roll it, Jon," she commanded.

Katie and Tony were bathed in the light of Jon's camera as he squinted through the viewfinder.

"Tell me, Katie Shannon," Beth said, sticking a microphone in Katie's face, "what was the most interesting thing that you did instead of watching television during the last two weeks?"

Everything that had happened during the TV turnoff raced through Katie's mind. She thought about her fight with Tony and her problems with Laura. Of course there had been some nice things, too—working on the turnoff with Willie and The Fabulous Five, playing Monopoly with her mother, and making up with Tony. But she didn't want to talk about any of those things on television.

"Oh, nothing special happened, really," Katie said.

Beth stared at Katie in disbelief. "You're kidding! That's all you have to say about the last two weeks?"

Katie shrugged.

Beth shook her head. "Kill that, Jon," she said. "We'll find someone else to interview."

Katie laughed and turned to Melanie. "Have you

watched any of your *Interns and Lovers* tapes, now that the turnoff is over?" she asked.

Melanie made a face. "Yes, and I almost died!"

"Why?" asked Katie.

"I watched last week's shows, and Sylvia was still in intensive care, hooked up to all those machines. She hadn't even regained consciousness! Then I checked the tapes for this week, too, and would you believe, *she's still in intensive care?* I ended up fast-forwarding through most of it, and the only thing that really happened was that her eyelids fluttered for the first time today." Melanie slapped her forehead. "I didn't miss a thing by not watching for two weeks."

"Well, at least you didn't pay Laura to watch the show for you," said Jana.

Melanie nodded.

Just then the band played a fanfare. The lights brightened, and Mr. Bell walked out onto the stage with Willie and Mrs. Karl. He held up his hands for quiet.

"Students of Wakeman Junior High," he began, "let me first introduce two ladies who had a great deal to do with the success of the Wakeman turnoff, Wilma Shannon and Mary Karl." The audience applauded.

"If it had not been for Mrs. Karl's hard work and

Mrs. Shannon's research and her articles on the problems of watching too much television, as well as her suggestion that Wakeman Junior High conduct a turnoff of its own, we wouldn't be having this party tonight!" The applause was even louder.

Katie felt a swelling of pride as she looked at her mother standing in the spotlight on the stage.

"Let me get right to the thing I know you're waiting to hear," said Mr. Bell, "the results of our competition with Branford Junior High."

There was a flurry of applause, and Mr. Bell smiled as he waited for it to stop.

"At the end of their one-week turnoff, sixty-four percent of the Branford students had not watched television. At the end of Wakeman's *two* weeks, *seventy-eight* percent of you had not watched TV, which means that Wakeman Junior High won!"

A cheer went up from the audience, and kids slapped each other's backs in congratulations. Katie beamed as Jana and Melanie hugged her.

Katie looked up at her mother. When she caught Willie's eye, she gave her a thumbs-up sign.

"Now," continued Mr. Bell, "since we have so many people who get certificates and awards, we've set up a table here on the stage. At your convenience, please come up and get them from Mrs. Shannon and Mrs.

Karl. Thank you all, students. Congratulations, Wakeman Junior High! We're proud of you."

"Isn't it great?" said Christie, who had wandered over with Beth, Dekeisha, and Mandy. "Wakeman won, and you had a lot to do with it, Katie."

"*We all* had a lot to do with it," said Katie. "Every one of you helped." She squeezed Tony's hand.

"One of the interesting things I found out as I interviewed people this evening," said Beth, "is how much everyone really enjoyed the turnoff. Lots of kids said they had a blast doing other things. I would never have expected that in the beginning."

A warm glow filled Katie as she realized just how worthwhile the TV turnoff had been. People had liked doing other things besides watching television, and they were paying more attention to *each other*, which was the most important thing of all.

As the party drew to a close, Katie looked up at Tony and asked, "What do you want to do for the rest of the evening?"

"Well . . . the Sox are playing the Angels on TV, and I thought we might . . ."

Katie swung and hit him on the shoulder.

Tony held up his hands in protest and grinned. "Hey, I'm only kidding, Your Honor. I'm only kidding."

CHAPTER

14

Christie finished the math test and skimmed back over the questions. Her answers looked correct. Sticking her pencil into her book bag, she walked to the front of the class past boys and girls still working hard on their papers.

"Egghead," whispered Richie Corrierro, as she walked by his desk.

"Quiet!" Mr. Snider said firmly. "No talking, or I'll have to give you a zero on the test."

Christie shot Richie a dirty look as she dropped the paper on the teacher's desk. Richie grinned devilishly back at her.

* * *

"Wow!" Melanie flopped down on the seat next to Christie in the cafeteria. "I just took an IQ test in social studies, and I think I flunked."

"You can't flunk an IQ test," said Christie. "That's not what they're for. All they do is give you some idea about how smart you are."

"Eeek! That's worse," replied Melanie. "What if I find out that I'm terminally stupid?"

"Don't be silly, Mel," said Jana. "You're not stupid."

"But what if the test says I am? I'm terrible at taking tests. I just know I got a zero on it. Everyone will find out, and I'll get teased."

"Everybody gets teased," said Christie. "I just got teased by Richie Corrierro because I finished a test before anyone else."

"Well, that's different," argued Melanie. "You're a genius, and he's just jealous."

"I'm not that smart. The test was just easy."

"For you, maybe," said Beth.

Christie rolled her eyes. It wasn't just because it was her. In most of her classes all you had to do was memorize things. If you were interested in what was going on and read a lot, they didn't teach you much. It was getting harder and harder to keep her mind on school, and to be teased because she got good grades was a *real* pain.

"Teasing is all the same," replied Christie with a sigh. "It gets old."

"Don't worry about it, Christie," said Katie. "Richie and his friends are just stupid. You don't need them, anyway."

"Yeah," added Beth brightly. "We're your friends, and we don't tease you for being brilliant. We love you in spite of it."

"You're all heart," said Christie, smiling.

"Truthfully," joined in Jana, "isn't that what The Fabulous Five's all about? We're friends forever, remember? No one can put any of us down as long as we have each other."

Christie smiled at her friend. Jana was right. Whenever any of them had a problem, the others would rush to help. As long as I've got Jana, Katie, Melanie, and Beth, nothing can bother me, she thought resolutely. As a matter of fact, nothing in the world can hurt me.

But what will Christie do if she finds out that she may not have The Fabulous Five to be friends with anymore? And what will happen if someone special encourages her to break rules? Read *The Fabulous Five #25: The Fabulous Five Minus One*, and find out.

ABOUT THE AUTHOR

Betsy Haynes, the daughter of a former news-woman, began scribbling poetry and short stories as soon as she learned to write. A serious writing career, however, had to wait until after her marriage and the arrival of her two children. But that early practice must have paid off, for within three months Mrs. Haynes had sold her first story. In addition to a number of magazine short stories and the Taffy Sinclair series, Mrs. Haynes is also the author of *The Great Mom Swap* and its sequel, *The Great Boyfriend Trap*. She lives in Marco Island, Florida, with her husband, who is also an author.

Taffy Sinclair is perfectly gorgeous and totally stuck-up. Ask her rival Jana Morgan or anyone else in the sixth grade of Mark Twain Elementary. Once you meet Taffy, life will **never** be the same.

Don't Miss Any of the Terrific Taffy Sinclair Titles from Betsy Haynes!

☐ 15819 **TAFFY GOES TO HOLLYWOOD** $2.95

☐ 15712 **THE AGAINST TAFFY SINCLAIR CLUB** $2.75

☐ 15693 **BLACKMAILED BY TAFFY SINCLAIR** $2.75

☐ 15604 **TAFFY SINCLAIR AND THE MELANIE MAKEOVER** $2.75

☐ 15644 **TAFFY SINCLAIR AND THE ROMANCE MACHINE DISASTER** $2.75

☐ 15714 **TAFFY SINCLAIR AND THE SECRET ADMIRER EPIDEMIC** $2.75

☐ 15713 **TAFFY SINCLAIR, BABY ASHLEY AND ME** $2.75

☐ 15647 **TAFFY SINCLAIR, QUEEN OF THE SOAPS** $2.75

☐ 15645 **TAFFY SINCLAIR STRIKES AGAIN** $2.75

☐ 15607 **THE TRUTH ABOUT TAFFY SINCLAIR** $2.75

Follow the adventures of Jana and the rest of **THE FABULOUS FIVE** in a new series by Betsy Haynes.